and the
UNUSUAL YAK

For Salome
J.S.

For Michael & Ben
C.E.

Reading Consultant: Prue Goodwin, Lecturer in literacy and children's books

ORCHARD BOOKS
338 Euston Road, London NW1 3BH
Orchard Books Australia
Level 17/207 Kent Street, Sydney, NSW 2000

First published in 2012
First paperback publication in 2013

ISBN 978 1 40831 332 9 (hardback)
ISBN 978 1 40831 340 4 (paperback)

Text © Justine Smith 2012
Illustrations © Clare Elsom 2012

A CIP catalogue record for this book is available from the British Library.

1 3 5 7 9 10 8 6 4 2 (hardback)
1 3 5 7 9 10 8 6 4 2 (paperback)

Printed in China

Orchard Books is a division of Hachette Children's Books,
an Hachette UK company.
www.hachette.co.uk

and the
UNUSUAL YAK

Justine Smith • Clare Elsom

ORCHARD

*Zak Zoo lives at Number One, Africa Avenue.
His mum and dad are away on
safari, so his animal family is looking
after him. Sometimes things get a little . . .*

. . . WILD!

Late one night, Tom the post-bird
delivered a letter to Zak Zoo.

Little green tent
The Snowfields
Siberia

Dear Zak,

We have sent you an unusual yak. He will arrive on Friday. Please take special care of him.

Love,

Mum and Dad

P.S. Are you eating your greens?

On Friday, Zak's best friend Mia came for breakfast.

"There is a big crate in your garden," she said.

"That will be my yak!" said Zak.

Zak and Mia went to look at the crate. It jumped and bumped. "He's a very lively yak," said Zak.

Inside the crate, the yak moaned
and groaned.

"He's not a very happy yak,"
said Mia.

The yak went quiet.

"Perhaps he's asleep," said Zak.

"Let's get him out," said Zak, and
he went to get his tools.

Zak opened up the crate.

"Hello, Mr Yak," he said politely.

The yak didn't reply.

Zak thought the yak might be
hungry after his long journey.
So he took him into the kitchen
for a snack.

After his snack, the yak went to lie down on the sofa. His shaggy coat dropped hair everywhere.

He was very messy and VERY

smelly!

Next, the yak went to look upstairs,
leaving dirty hoof-prints everywhere.
He seemed happy with his new home.

The yak did an awful lot of

unusual things.

That night he sang to the moon.

The yak really was unusually rude. He never said "please" or "thank you".

He liked to sit in front of the open
fridge, and he never helped with
the washing up.

He liked to take cold baths.

He liked to make milkshakes with
ice cream.

Poor Nanny Hilda spent all her
time cleaning up!

Zak wrote to his parents.

Dear Mum and Dad,

The yak has arrived safely. He is unusual, all right!
I am doing my best to take care of him.

Love,
Zak
P.S. Don't worry. I ate a green bean last week.

Zak wondered how he could take better care of the yak. He searched the internet and found out that yaks live in snowy places.

"I think this yak is too hot," said Zak.

"I think you're right," said Mia.

It was obvious that the yak needed to cool down.

"I know just what to do,"

said Zak.

He drew a picture of his idea.

Zak got to work outside, building a new, cool house for the yak.

The yak didn't say "thank you".

He was far too rude for that.

The yak moved into his new
house, but he was still too hot.

Zak went to bed worried. But that night a strong wind blew through the tree outside his window. It gave him another idea.

He jumped out of bed and started
work at once.

Zak rebuilt the yak's house high in the tree, where it was cool and breezy. And then something very unusual happened.

"Thank you," said the yak.

Written by Justine Smith • Illustrated by Clare Elsom

Zak Zoo and the School Hullabaloo   978 1 40831 329 9

Zak Zoo and the Peculiar Parcel   978 1 40831 330 5

Zak Zoo and the Seaside SOS   978 1 40831 331 2

Zak Zoo and the Unusual Yak   978 1 40831 332 9

Zak Zoo and the Hectic House   978 1 40831 333 6

Zak Zoo and the Baffled Burglar   978 1 40831 334 3

Zak Zoo and the TV Crew   978 1 40831 335 0

Zak Zoo and the Birthday Bang   978 1 40831 336 7

All priced at £8.99

Orchard Books are available from all good bookshops,
or can be ordered from our website: www.orchardbooks.co.uk,
or telephone 01235 827702, or fax 01235 827703.

Prices and availability are subject to change.